Don Quixote
and
Sancho Panza

Don Quixote and Sancho Panza

ADAPTED BY

MARGARET HODGES

FROM

DON QUIXOTE OF LA MANCHA

BY MIGUEL DE CERVANTES SAAVEDRA

◆ ◆ ◆

ILLUSTRATED BY

STEPHEN MARCHESI

CHARLES SCRIBNER'S SONS • NEW YORK
Maxwell Macmillan Canada • Toronto
Maxwell Macmillan International
New York • Oxford • Singapore • Sydney

To Rocinante and Dapple

Charles Scribner's Sons Books for Young Readers
Macmillan Publishing Company, 866 Third Avenue, New York, NY 10022

Maxwell Macmillan Canada, Inc.
1200 Eglinton Avenue East, Suite 200, Don Mills, Ontario M3C 3N1

Macmillan Publishing Company is part of the
Maxwell Communication Group of Companies.

First Edition   10   9   8   7   6   5   4   3   2   1
Printed in the United States of America

Library of Congress Cataloging-in-Publication Data
Hodges, Margaret.
   Don Quixote and Sancho Panza from Miguel de Cervantes Saavedra's
Don Quixote of La Mancha / adapted by Margaret Hodges. — 1st ed.
      p.   cm.
   Summary: An abridged version of the adventures of an eccentric
country gentleman and his faithful companion who set out as knight
and squire of old to right wrongs and punish evil.
ISBN 0-684-19235-7
[1. Knights and knighthood—Fiction.   2. Spain—Fiction.]
I. Cervantes Saavedra, Miguel de, 1547–1616.   Don Quixote.   II. Title.
PZ7.H664Do   1992   [Fic]—dc20   90–24098

Cervantes on his galley sets the sword back in the sheath
(Don John of Austria rides homeward with a wreath).
And he sees across a weary land a straggling road in Spain,
Up which a lean and foolish knight forever rides in vain.

G. K. CHESTERTON: *Lepanto*

CONTENTS

INTRODUCING THE READER
TO TWO TRAVELERS

The Mexican author Carlos Fuentes has said that when Don Quixote mounted his horse and rode away from his village, the modern world began. Is *Don Quixote* the world's first modern novel? Is it the world's greatest novel? Many writers have answered yes to both questions. What a pity then if we have not read at least a few of the adventures of the gentleman from La Mancha and his devoted squire, Sancho Panza, who is as important as the knight he serves. That is why I have called this selection of their adventures *Don Quixote and Sancho Panza*. Nor should their steeds go unthanked. This book is dedicated to Rocinante and Dapple.

Don Quixote set forth on his travels through Spain obsessed with what he had read in books about chivalry. Because of those books he did not meet with events the way other people did. He had stepped back into the past and saw things "through a glass, darkly." (In *Through the Looking-Glass,* Alice's White Knight is not quite like a real knight. For example, like Don Quixote, he keeps falling off his horse.)

But if Don Quixote is not a real knight, what is real? A great Spanish writer, Miguel de Unamuno, has said that in order to see reality, inside as well as outside, we need to have a "looking-glass view." And when we look into *Don Quixote* we see ourselves mirrored there. That is why the adventures of Don Quixote and Sancho Panza are always fresh and new.

It is often said that we should read *Don Quixote* at least three times; in youth, middle age, and old age. The don is like a child playing at knighthood, though he is two generations too old for child's play. Who but a child—or a madman—would ride off to battle wearing a cardboard visor and a helmet tied on by ribbons? Who else would see Rocinante, a mere bag of skin and bones, as "the mirror of steeds"? The don's very name, which we pronounce Kē-hōt-ē, has passed into the English language as *quixote*, and *quixotic*, meaning foolishly impractical in the pursuit of ideals. Yet the impractical old fool, by seeing himself as a strong and valiant knight, becomes so.

Cervantes himself (1547–1616) is mirrored in *Don Quixote*. Cervantes had been a good soldier in his day, and nothing could ever take away the knowledge that he had been brave in combat. In the great naval battle of Lepanto (1571) when Don John of Austria commanded an allied fleet against the Turks, Cervantes, sick with a fever, demanded and was given a post of extreme danger. He was shot twice in the chest and a third bullet maimed his left hand, "for the greater glory of the right," as he said. He was taken captive and spent five years as a slave in Africa. He was later sent to prison at least three times on various charges. He may have written some of *Don Quixote* in a prison cell, and other chapters were written at Valladolid in a house that still stands. Part I appeared in 1605. It brought fame, but little profit to Cervantes. Part II was published in 1615. Poor, broken in body, though not in spirit, the author died on April 23, 1616, the day of Shakespeare's death.

The best mirror we can find in which to see Cervantes's hero is in the long-suffering Sancho Panza, who understands his master all too well, just as Don Quixote understands Sancho. We cannot think of the one without the other, the fat and the lean, the short and the tall, the worldly and the otherworldly, different in every way, yet oddly in harmony.

Aside from the ever present Sancho, the person closest to Don Quixote, and the one he sees most clearly, is one who is not there at all. This is "Dulcinea del Toboso," really a coarse farm girl, Aldonza Lorenzo, with whose pretty face he had once been smitten. In his mind's eye the don sees her as the very mirror of all the faraway princesses of romance. She is a most satisfactory ideal, for as he sees her, she will never change, and can never grow old, while he remains the young cavalier for whom every goose is a swan. When that image departs, when the mirror is empty, he will die. Cervantes gives us tears as well as laughter, but he wants our laughter more than our tears, except at the end when we must say farewell.

If we read a little of *Don Quixote* in our youth, it is usually the adventure with the windmills, and no more. In middle age, with that memory in mind, we may buy an abridged version and enjoy every chapter, planning to read the entire novel some day when there is more time. Perhaps old age brings that time, and it may be the best time to read all of *Don Quixote*. It will wait for us patiently, knowing that it has had the praise of the best critics for four hundred years, this book of the whole Spanish people and of all humanity. At the beginning of Part II, Don Quixote's friend the student comes to see him and tells him that a book has been written about him. "Children turn its leaves, young people read it, grown-ups understand it, and old folks commend it. In a word, it is so well thumbed and read and learned by heart by people of all sorts that no sooner do they see any lean hack than they cry out: 'There goes Rocinante.'"

In trying to capture the flavor of Cervantes, I have compared all available translations and found Samuel Putnam's the most helpful. I also liked an abridged version translated and edited by Walter Starkie. It pleases me that *Don Quixote and Sancho Panza* is appearing on the 500th anniversary of the voyage of Christopher Columbus, who brought the Spanish language to the New World.

ONE

A KNIGHT RIDES FORTH

In the days when soldiers already carried muskets filled with bullets and gunpowder, and handsome knights in shining armor no longer rode out to rescue damsels in distress, an elderly Spanish gentleman lived in a village in the region of La Mancha. I can't remember the name of the village; it doesn't matter. The gentleman was far from handsome, being too tall, thin as a rail, and having a long, lean, sallow face with a gray beard. I'm not sure what his real name was, but he called himself Don Quixote of La Mancha, though his family was not of the highest class and he really had no right to the title of Don.

Most nights he dined on cold stew, ate lentil soup on Fridays, and sometimes a pigeon as a treat on Sundays. However, he liked to think of himself as a knight because, except for a little hunting now and then, he spent all his time reading old romances and books of chivalry. He lived very quietly, cared for by his housekeeper, who was over forty years old; a niece, who was under twenty; and a farm lad, who tended Don Quixote's few acres of land and saddled his horse, an old nag as skinny as his master.

At last, from spending all his days and nights reading about knights and enchantments, battles, challenges, wounds, and hopeless love for beautiful princesses, Don Quixote went out of his mind on the subject of chivalry, though remaining perfectly sane in other ways, and decided to roam the world on horseback as a knight-errant in armor, looking for adventures and righting wrongs.

He shined up some old pieces of armor that had once belonged to his great-grandfather, borrowed a shield from a neighbor, and spent a week making a cardboard visor to attach to a helmet of the kind that common soldiers had once worn. When he tested the visor and found that it could not stand even one thrust of his sword, he added a few strips of iron to fit inside across his face. Then he tied on his helmet with ribbons and, quite satisfied, went off to look at his nag in the stable.

The animal was nothing but skin and bones, and its hooves were badly cracked. Still, Don Quixote thought that his horse was sure to become as famous as he himself would be, and therefore should have a good name. He spent four days thinking and finally decided on Rocinante, which sounded well and had a meaning, "First and Foremost Nag in the World."

Now that he had a suit of armor and a name for himself and for his horse, Don Quixote lacked only one thing, a lady to love, for without a ladylove a knight-errant was nothing. As the story goes, he had once cast his eye on a good-looking farm girl in the nearby village of El Toboso. She did not know that he had ever looked at her, but he decided to do noble deeds in her honor and to call her "Dulcinea del Toboso," a name which he thought to be both musical and unusual.

With his preparations completed, Don Quixote could not wait to begin righting wrongs and doing justice. One morning before dawn of a hot day in July, he armed himself from head to foot, mounted Rocinante, put his makeshift helmet on his head, fastened his shield on his arm, seized his lance, and rode out through the gate of his stable yard.

But no sooner was he in the open country than he had a terrible thought. He remembered that, according to the rules of chivalry, he could not fight against any knight until he himself had been made a knight. Still, he could be knighted by the first knight he met, as often happened in the books he had read. With this in mind, he became calmer and let Rocinante choose the road to add to the true spirit of adventure.

The sun came up hot enough to melt his brains, if he had any, but he traveled on all day without meeting any adventures. By nightfall he and his horse were tired out and half dead with hunger, so he looked about for a castle where he could rest and eat supper. Not far from the road he saw an inn. Now everything that he saw looked to him like something he had read about in his books of chivalry, so instead of an inn he saw a castle with turrets and towers of shining silver as well as a drawbridge and a moat.

Near the inn he pulled Rocinante to a halt, expecting a dwarf to appear on the battlements and blow a trumpet blast to announce the arrival of a knight. But since the dwarf was slow in coming and Rocinante was in a hurry to get to the stable, Don Quixote rode on toward the inn. There he saw two girls who were traveling with mule drivers and had stopped for the night. At this moment a swineherd came along and blew his horn to round up his hogs. Don Quixote took him to be the dwarf he was expecting, so he rode up to the inn door and spoke gently to the girls, whom he saw as beautiful damsels or highborn ladies.

They seemed to be frightened by the sight of a man in full armor, so he raised his visor, showing his wrinkled face, covered with dust, and said, "Do not be afraid, your ladyships. I am a knight who would not wrong any lady, much less such noble maidens as you."

He was offended when the girls burst into a roar of laughter, and there is no knowing what he might have said next if the innkeeper had not come out. He was a fat, jolly man and would have laughed with the girls at the sight of the awkward figure in odd bits of armor, but he was afraid of the lance and said politely, "Sir Knight, if you are looking for a lodging, we can give you everything you want here, except a bed."

Thinking that the landlord was a knight, Don Quixote replied courteously that a knight needed no comforts except his armor and no rest except combat.

"Then come in," said the landlord. "A night in this house will keep you awake."

Don Quixote dismounted with the help of the innkeeper, nearly falling from hunger, since he had not eaten all day. He told his host to take good care of Rocinante because he was the best horse in the world. The innkeeper doubted it, but he stabled the old nag. When he returned, he found the girls removing the knight's armor, while Don Quixote recited poetry to them, calling them "fair ladies" and "damsels" and "princesses." They could not remove his helmet. He had fastened it on by tying green ribbons into tight and complicated knots and would not let them be cut.

The girls placed a table for him at the door of the inn and brought him a piece of badly cooked codfish and some moldy black bread, which they fed to him through the metal strips that covered his face. For drink, the innkeeper hollowed out a reed, put one end in the knight's mouth, and poured wine in at the other. All this Don Quixote bore very patiently rather than let them cut the ribbons of his helmet. He wore it all night long.

Only one thing troubled him. After his meager supper he shut himself up in the stable with the landlord and fell to his knees, saying, "I will never get up unless you grant me a boon. Tomorrow morning, dub me a knight. Tonight I will place my armor on the altar in the chapel of your castle and keep watch over it, as knights must do."

The innkeeper had now decided that Don Quixote was crazy, so he said that although he was a knight himself, he had torn down his old chapel to build a new one. In a case like this, he said, a knight could keep watch over his armor anywhere, even in a barnyard. He asked Don Quixote if he had any money.

"Not a penny," said the knight. "In stories, knights never carry any money."

"You are wrong," said the landlord. "Even if authors do not speak of it, knights always had money and clean shirts. They also carried a little box of ointment to heal their wounds, unless a maiden or a dwarf came flying through the air to heal them with a flask of magic water. Otherwise, knights had squires to carry their money and other necessities. In the future, be sure to travel with some money."

Don Quixote promised to do so and carried his armor into the barnyard, where he saw a stone trough used for watering animals. He laid his armor on the trough and began to pace solemnly up and down in front of it, carrying his lance. Just then one of the mule drivers came to water his mules. He was about to move the armor when Don Quixote shouted, "Don't touch the arms of the bravest knight in the world, if you value your life."

The mule driver paid no attention but hurled the armor away, upon which Don Quixote raised his eyes to heaven, asked Dulcinea's blessing, and dealt the mule driver such a blow on the head that the man fell to the ground. Then Don Quixote put his armor back on the water trough and resumed his pacing. Some time later a second mule driver came out. He was about to move Don Quixote's armor from the trough when the knight, without warning, again raised his lance and split the man's head open. At the sound of this commotion, everyone came running out, and the other mule drivers threw stones at Don Quixote. The landlord told them to stop because this was a madman, while Don Quixote kept shouting that they were all villains and traitors. He sounded so fearless that they were terrified. They stopped pelting him and carried away the two wounded men, whereupon Don Quixote quietly went back to watching his armor.

The innkeeper was tired of his guest's nonsense and decided to put an end to it. He told Don Quixote that according to the rules of chivalry two hours were enough for keeping watch over armor. He

only needed a slap on the neck and one on the shoulder to be dubbed a knight. Don Quixote believed all this and said he was ready. The innkeeper then brought out the account book in which he jotted down sales of straw and barley, and began to mumble as if he were reading prayers. Don Quixote knelt down and the landlord took his sword and gave him a good whack on the neck and another on the shoulder. One of the girls then girded on his sword and the other put on his spurs at top speed, while he thanked them and the landlord in flowery language.

The innkeeper was so glad to see him go that he did not care whether or not Don Quixote paid his bill, and the knight was so impatient to be off in search of adventures that he saddled Rocinante and rode off. Remembering the innkeeper's advice, he headed toward home for money and clean shirts. The old horse was glad to be going

in the direction of his own stable, and he and Don Quixote were in high spirits. As he went along, the knight thought of a farmer, a poor man with a family, who would make a good squire.

Two miles farther on the road they met some traders from Toledo on their way to buy silk. There were six of them with four servants and three mule drivers.

Don Quixote thought that he should confront them all, as bold knights did in storybooks, so he settled himself in his stirrups, grasped his lance, raised his shield, and stopped in the middle of the road, calling out, "Go no farther, unless you will confess that Dulcinea del Toboso is the most beautiful lady in the world!"

Both from his looks and his words the merchants saw that Don Quixote was crazy, and one of them who was a joker, and clever, said, "Sir Knight, we don't know who this lady is. Show her to us, and if she is as beautiful as you say, we will at once agree with you."

"If I showed her to you," said Don Quixote, "what would be the point of your agreeing with me? You must believe and agree without

seeing her. If not, come and do battle with me, monsters that you are. Come one by one, or all together."

"Sir Knight," answered the merchant, "it goes against our conscience to swear to something that we don't know. Show us even a tiny picture of the lady, and we will agree with you, no matter how ugly she looks."

"No indeed!" cried Don Quixote, in a towering rage. "And you shall pay for those words!"

He lowered his lance and rode forward with such fury that things would have gone badly for the merchant if Rocinante had not stumbled and fallen in the road. His master went rolling over the ground and could not get to his feet as he struggled with his lance, his shield, the spurs, the helmet, and the heavy armor, crying out, "Wait, cowards! It was my horse's fault, not mine, that I fell."

For an answer, one of the mule drivers broke the lance into pieces and splintered them on the wretched knight. At last the merchants said that enough was enough, but the fellow went on beating Don Quixote until he himself was tired, while the knight kept bellowing threats to heaven and earth and those villainous bandits, as he called the merchants. When they were gone, he tried again to get up, but if he could not have done it when he was hale and hearty, how could he do it now that he was pounded to pieces? Yet, as he saw it, knights had to expect such misfortunes, and it was all his horse's fault, so he lay there reciting poems about knights and ladies until a peasant from his own village happened to pass by with his donkey.

Amazed at what he saw and heard, he took off the knight's battered visor, wiped the dust from his face, and knew who he was. He removed the heavy armor and managed to get Don Quixote astride the donkey. When he had gathered up all the arms, even the splinters of the lance, and tied them to Rocinante's back, he led the two animals toward the village. Don Quixote recited poetry all the way about knights taken prisoner and other such nonsense. The peasant saw that he was out of his wits and wanted to be rid of him, but he kindly waited until after dark so that the villagers would not see their neighbor in such a sad condition, mounted on a donkey.

At Don Quixote's house everything was in an uproar. The village priest and the barber were there, both great friends of Don Quixote, and the housekeeper was shouting, "Three days now he has been gone, horse, lance, shield, armor, and all. Those cursed books of chivalry have turned his head. He has been talking to himself about becoming a knight and going off on adventures. The devil take those books!"

The niece agreed. She said to the barber, "It is true. My uncle used to sit for days and nights at a time reading those wicked stories. Then he would toss the books away, draw his sword, and slash at the walls until he was tired out, saying that he had just killed four giants. He would tell us that his sweat was blood from his wounds, and he would drink a whole jug of water. He said it was a precious drink given to him by his friend, a magician, and it had healed his wounds. Then he would be calm again. I blame myself for not having told you. Perhaps you could have cured him of his madness by burning those cursed books."

"I agree," said the priest. "We will burn them tomorrow before anyone else reads them and goes mad like our poor knight."

Just then they heard the peasant shouting for the door to be opened and ranting about knights and wounds and captives. Everyone rushed out, and, embracing Don Quixote, carried him in, while he kept asking for a witch to heal the wounds he had got in a fight with ten giants. They gave him food and put him to bed, where he fell fast asleep.

TWO

THE BATTLE WITH THE WINDMILLS

The next morning, while Don Quixote was still sleeping, the priest and the barber came to the house. The knight's niece gave them the keys to the room where he kept his books, and they went in with the housekeeper. They found more than a hundred big volumes and many smaller ones. The priest took them from the shelves, one by one, and handed them to the housekeeper, who threw them out of the window into the courtyard. While they were at this work, Don Quixote woke up and began to rave about knights, enchantments, and revenge, but they gave him another meal, and he fell asleep again.

That night the housekeeper burned all of Don Quixote's books, good and bad alike. As the saying goes, "The saints pay for the sinners." During two days, while Don Quixote stayed in bed, the priest and the barber walled up the book room, covering the doorway with plaster. When the knight got up and wanted to go to his study, he could not even find the room. He went over the house, feeling all the walls with his hands. At last he asked the housekeeper what had become of his book room. "Book room?" she replied. "What book room? The devil has carried it off, and all the books, too."

"Not the devil, but an enchanter," said the niece. "He came into your book room one night, riding on a dragon. I don't know what he did there, but he left in a cloud of smoke, and your room and your books disappeared."

"I know that enchanter," said Don Quixote, "and I will defeat him yet."

"Of course, dear uncle," said the niece, "but why not stay peacefully at home instead of roaming about looking for trouble?"

At this, the knight began to grow angry, so his niece and the housekeeper decided not to argue with him. For two weeks he stayed at home and had pleasant conversations with the priest and the barber about the need for knights to save the world. They let him have his way rather than send him into a fit of rage.

All this while, Don Quixote was visiting a farmer, an honest creature, but not very bright. His name was Sancho Panza, and he was as short and fat as the knight was tall and lean. Don Quixote talked to him so much and made so many promises that at last he persuaded this bumpkin to go along as his squire, for he told the unlucky fellow that they were sure to win an island in their adventures and battles, and Sancho could be the governor of it. As a result, Sancho Panza left his wife and children and loaded his gray donkey, Dapple, with saddlebags full of all that a knight-errant and his squire might need. Don Quixote said that he had never read of a squire mounted on a donkey, but that he would give him the horse of the first wicked knight he overcame in battle.

One night, unseen by anyone, neither wife nor children, housekeeper nor niece, Don Quixote and Sancho set forth, Sancho riding

along on Dapple with saddlebags and a full wineskin, his mind fixed on becoming governor of the island that his master had promised him. Don Quixote rejoiced because he was now ready to become famous by bringing back the happiest of times when knights-errant defended kingdoms single-handed, protected damsels, rescued orphans, punished the proud, and rewarded the humble.

"Sir Knight," said Sancho, "don't forget about that island. No matter how big it is, I'll be able to govern it."

"Never fear," said Don Quixote. "Knights of old often made their squires wait for years to be rewarded with some valley or province, but I may conquer a kingdom by the end of this week, and I might easily give you more than I have promised, and make you a king."

"And if I become king, would my wife become queen, and my children princes?" asked Sancho.

"Of course," said Don Quixote.

"My wife wouldn't be worth two cents as a queen," replied Sancho. "She would do better as a countess, and even then, God help her."

"Leave it in God's hands," said the knight, "but don't be satisfied with any title less than governor."

Just then they came in sight of thirty or forty windmills which stood on the plain where they were riding. As soon as Don Quixote saw them, he said, "Fortune is with us, my friend. Yonder are thirty or more huge giants whom I intend to kill. With the spoils of war we will be rich, for God will bless us in a righteous cause."

"What giants?" said Sancho.

"Over there," replied the knight. "Some of them have arms six miles long."

"Those things aren't giants," answered Sancho. "They are windmills. They don't have arms, but sails that whirl around in the wind and turn the millstones."

"You have no experience in adventures," said Don Quixote. "They are giants. If you are afraid, go off and say your prayers while I fight them single-handed."

Sancho warned him again, but Don Quixote paid no attention. He dug his spurs into Rocinante's sides and rode to the attack, shouting, "Don't run, cowards! It is all of you against one lone knight."

At that moment a little wind rose and the great wings began to move. Don Quixote shouted, "I'll make you pay, no matter how many arms you shake at me."

Saying this, he prayed for the help of his lady Dulcinea in his great danger. Then he covered himself with his shield and galloped forward to attack the nearest windmill, thrusting his lance into a sail. But the wind twisted the lance so hard that it broke into pieces, dragging him and his horse to the ground and sending him rolling over and over across the plain.

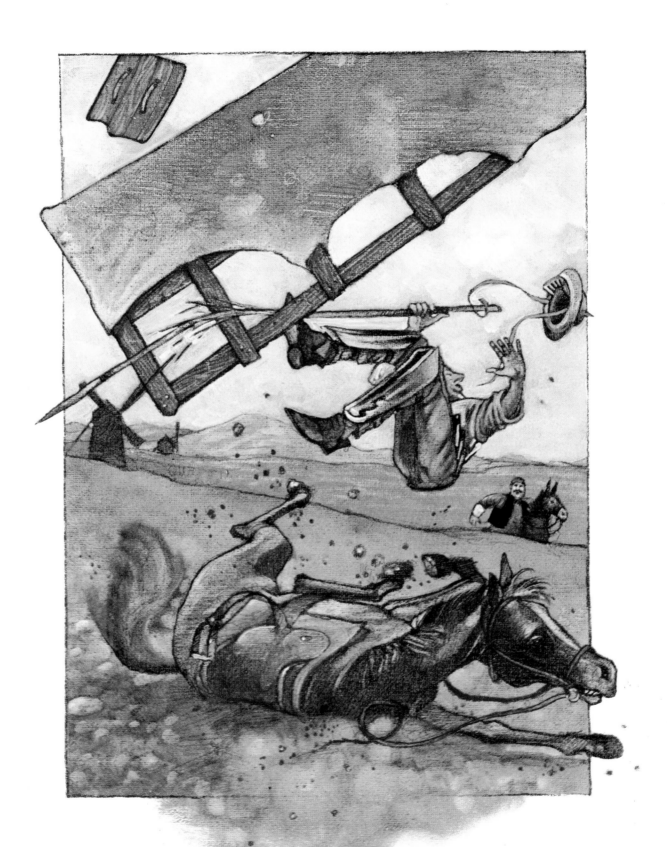

Sancho Panza rushed to help him as fast as Dapple could gallop and found the knight in a state of shock from his fall, unable to move.

"God help us!" said Sancho. "Didn't I tell you that those were windmills? Anyone could see that, unless he had windmills on his brain."

"Hold your peace, dear Sancho," answered Don Quixote. "In war there are constant changes. I am convinced that the magician who stole my room and my books changed those giants into windmills to deprive me of my glory. But in the end, my good sword will prevail over his evil arts."

"As God wills," said Sancho, and helped his master back on Rocinante, who stood there with one shoulder half out of joint.

So, talking of their adventure, they rode along the highway. The only thing that grieved Don Quixote was the loss of his lance. "I remember reading about a Spanish knight who lost his sword in battle," he told Sancho. "He tore a branch from an oak tree and performed great feats of valor with it. I will get a branch like his and do such deeds with it that you will think yourself lucky to be with me."

"As God wills," replied Sancho. "I believe everything you say, but sit up a little straighter in your saddle. You seem to be slipping down on one side, no doubt because of your fall."

"No doubt," said Don Quixote, "but a knight is not allowed to complain, even if his insides are dropping out."

"Does this business of not complaining apply to squires, too?" asked Sancho.

Don Quixote laughed and said that a squire could complain as much as he liked. There were no rules against it. Sancho then said that it was time to eat. The knight replied that he was not hungry, but that a squire could eat whenever he liked. Sancho made himself comfortable on his donkey, took food out of the saddlebags, and jogged along after Don Quixote. Eating as he rode, and taking gulps out of the wineskin, he decided that going on adventures was at least better than working.

They spent that night under some trees, from one of which Don Quixote tore off a dead branch. On the end of it he stuck the iron point from the old lance that had been broken. Then he lay down, but he did not sleep, because he had read in his books that knights often lay awake all night thinking of their ladies. Not so with Sancho Panza. His stomach was full, and he slept like a log until morning. Even then Don Quixote had to wake him. There was not much left in the wineskin, but the knight wanted no breakfast. Thinking of pleasant memories was enough for him.

About three in the afternoon they came to a place where the

road went through a pass in the hills. "Here, brother Sancho, is a place where we are sure to have adventures," said Don Quixote, "but even if you see me in great danger, don't draw your sword to defend me if my enemies are knights. By the laws of chivalry, only a knight can fight against knights."

"You can be sure that I will obey you," said Sancho. "I am very peaceable and don't like to get into other people's quarrels. But if anyone attacks me, I won't trouble myself about those laws, since both divine and human law allow a man to defend himself."

"I agree," said Don Quixote, "but when it comes to defending me against knights, you will have to control yourself."

"I promise," said Sancho. "I will keep that law as strictly as I keep the Sabbath."

THREE

SANCHO'S STORY

S o Don Quixote and Sancho Panza rode on together day after day, up hill and down dale, through fair weather and foul. Whenever they came to a crossroads, Don Quixote let Rocinante choose the direction in which they should go. Within a very few months they thought they had traveled a long way, for everywhere they went they got into trouble.

As a consequence, Don Quixote and Sancho became so famous that a book was written about them. Rocinante, too, became so famous that when people saw any worn-out nag, they would cry out, "There goes Rocinante!" No one like Don Quixote had ever been seen before. Most people thought that he was insane because everything that he saw looked to him like something from a story in one of his books. A few said he was wise, except on the subject of chivalry. Some laughed at him and played tricks on him, some tried to help him. As for Sancho, he could not make up his mind whether Don Quixote was the greatest

knight in the world and would some day make him governor of that island, or whether he himself was a fool for following a fool.

Whenever Don Quixote saw someone or something that looked to him like a foe, he put Rocinante to a feeble trot and rode against the enemy. When he was bruised, battered, and beaten, as almost always happened, the horse never stirred from his master's side, such was his well-bred loyalty. Meanwhile, Sancho usually climbed the best tree he could find, or hid under Dapple to be out of harm's way.

Sometimes, when they were lucky, they found inns where they could spend the night; Don Quixote said they were castles. On those nights there would be a stable and fodder for Rocinante and Dapple. But more often Sancho went sound asleep under a tree, while Don Quixote slept leaning against the trunk, or kept vigil in his saddle, as knights had done in days of old. The horse and the donkey stood all night, Rocinante's long neck resting on that of Dapple.

One night they were crossing a meadow, so dark that they went on foot, Don Quixote leading Rocinante by the reins, and Sancho at his side, leading Dapple by his halter. They had emptied the wineskin and were very thirsty, when they were cheered by the sound of water falling on rocks. But Sancho heard something else that frightened him, the sound of heavy thuds and of clanking chains. The noise in the darkness and the ghostly whispering of wind in the trees all added to Sancho's fear because he had no idea what they were.

But Don Quixote leaped onto Rocinante's back, brandished his spear, and said, "Friend, I am the hero born in this Iron Age to bring back the Golden Age, to face dangers and do mighty deeds. Notice, loyal and faithful squire, the darkness of this night, the mysterious sounds in these trees, the fearful noise of the waters, which seem to fall from the mountains of the moon, and that thumping that pounds in our ears. Any of these would put fear into the god of war himself, yet they only rouse my courage and make my heart leap with desire to ride forth on this adventure, no matter how difficult it may be. So tighten Rocinante's girth, and God be with you! If I do not return in three days, go home, and tell Dulcinea that her knight died undertaking deeds worthy of her."

Sancho began to weep, saying, "Master, I don't know why you want to get into this terrible adventure. It is night, no one can see us, and we can turn around and get out of here. Never mind if we don't drink for three days. Many a time our priest has said in his sermons, 'He who goes looking for trouble finds it.' And I, sir, left my home and wife and children to come with you, expecting to be better off, not worse, and just as I was looking forward to that wretched island that you have so often promised me, you say you are going to leave me all alone in this desolate place, miles from any other human being. For God's sake, wait at least until morning."

But Don Quixote answered, "Never let it be said that tears or prayers kept me from doing my duty as a knight. So tighten Rocinante's girth, Sancho, and stay here. I will soon return, alive or dead."

Seeing that his master's mind was made up, Sancho decided to use his wits. While tightening the horse's girth, he also tied Dapple's halter around Rocinante's two front feet, so that when Don Quixote tried to ride away, he could only move by short jumps.

Seeing that his trick had worked, Sancho said, "Ah, sir, heaven has taken pity on me and kept Rocinante from moving. Let me entertain you with a story to make the time pass until daybreak, unless you would rather sleep."

"Sleep yourself, if you want to," said Don Quixote. "You are a born sleeper. But knights do not rest in the midst of danger."

"Don't be angry, good master," said Sancho. Still terrified by the thumping sounds, he took hold of Don Quixote's saddle and leaned

against him for comfort as he began: "I hope I can remember this story, because it's one of the best. Once upon a time—may good things come to us and evil to him who goes looking for it—that's how they started their stories in ancient times, and it fits us like a ring on a finger, meaning that you must stay here quietly and not go looking for danger."

"Get on with your story, Sancho," said Don Quixote.

"Well, then," said Sancho, "pay attention and don't interrupt. In a village in Estremadura there lived a shepherd who kept goats. I mean he was a goatherd. And this shepherd or goatherd was named Lope Ruiz and this Lope Ruiz was in love with a shepherd girl whose name was Torralba and this shepherd girl called Torralba was the daughter of a rich herdsman and this rich herdsman—"

Don Quixote interrupted again. "If that is how you are going to tell your story, saying everything twice, you will still be telling it two days from now. Tell it straightforward, or not at all."

"Where I live," said Sancho, "stories are always told as I'm telling, and I can't learn a new way now."

"Tell it as you like, then," said Don Quixote. "I can't help listening."

"And so," Sancho went on, "as I said, this shepherd fell in love with the shepherdess Torralba, who was a plump, jolly girl, and rather mannish. She had a slight mustache—I can see her now."

"You mean you knew her?" asked Don Quixote.

"I didn't know her," replied Sancho, "but the man who told me the story swore that it was true so that when I told it I could swear that I had seen it all. So, as time went on, the devil, who never sleeps, brought it about that the love the shepherd had for the shepherdess turned to hatred. And the reason was, according to gossip, that she gave him reason to be jealous and he decided to leave that country and go where he would never see her again. But when Torralba found that he didn't love her anymore, she fell in love with him, though she had never loved him before."

"That's the way with women," said Don Quixote. "Go on, Sancho."

"So the shepherd did as he had decided to do. He got his goats together and set out from Estremadura on his way to Portugal. When Torralba heard about it, she set out after him, barefoot, with a pilgrim staff in her hand and a knapsack around her neck, in which they say she had a piece of a mirror and a broken comb and some kind of lotion for her face. But whatever she carried, I can't find out now. I will just tell you that the story says the shepherd and his flock came to the Guadiana River, which at that time of year was swollen and almost overflowing its banks, and there was no boat or anyone to ferry him and his goats across. This worried him because he could see Torralba coming and he knew she would annoy him by crying and pleading. However, he saw a fisherman with a little boat just big enough to hold one man and one goat. So he spoke to the man and he agreed to take the shepherd and his three hundred goats across. The fisherman got into the boat and took one goat over. Then he came back and got another one and came back and got another one—you must keep track of the goats that the fisherman rowed across the river because if you forget a single one, I can't go on with the story.

"So I'll go on and tell you that the landing place was very muddy and slippery and it took the fisherman a good while each time but he came back for another goat and another and another."

"So he rowed them all across," said Don Quixote. "Don't keep coming and going like that or it will take you a year to get them all on the other side."

"How many have got across so far?" asked Sancho.

"How should I know?" said Don Quixote.

"There, what did I tell you?" said Sancho. "You were supposed to count. Well, that's the end of the story. I can't go on with it."

"Why not?" asked Don Quixote. "Is it so important to know exactly how many goats have crossed that if you miss one you can't go on?"

"No, sir," answered Sancho, "but when I asked you how many goats had got across and you said you didn't know, everything I was going to say went out of my head, though the rest of the story was very funny and you would have laughed."

"Well, I never heard anything like it," said Don Quixote, "though coming from you, I shouldn't have been surprised. Those thumping sounds must have addled your brains."

"Maybe so," said Sancho, "but as for my story, it ends when you lose count of the goats."

Master and servant spent the night in conversation. When Sancho saw that day was about to dawn, he carefully untied Rocinante, who began to paw the ground. Don Quixote then repeated his instructions and farewells, saying that he had left a will by which Sancho's wages would be paid if his master was killed in combat and that if he came back alive, Sancho could be sure of getting his island. Sancho burst into tears and determined not to leave his master. As Don Quixote rode off in the direction from which the ceaseless and frightful noises still came, Sancho followed on foot, leading Dapple by the bridle.

Before long they came to some high rocks from which a waterfall plunged down into a little meadow. Nearby stood some ramshackle huts. Don Quixote implored his lady Dulcinea to aid him and rode forward, while Sancho peered fearfully between Rocinante's legs to get a glimpse of the danger. They soon saw what had kept them in terror and suspense all night. The hammering sound and the clanking came from the huts and was nothing but the hammers of a fulling mill that worked by waterpower.

Don Quixote hung his head in shame, but when Sancho exploded with laughter, he could not help smiling, too. That made Sancho laugh even harder and imitate his master's words, " 'I am the hero born in this Iron Age to bring back the Golden Age, to face dangers and do mighty deeds.' " And he went on repeating all that the knight had said when they first heard the noises.

Don Quixote was furious when he saw that Sancho was making fun of him, and he gave him two whacks with his lance.

Sancho was afraid of what he might do next, so he said, "Please, master, I was only joking."

"But I am not joking," said Don Quixote. "How was I to know whether those noises were not made by giants? I never saw a fulling mill in my life. Turn those hammers into giants and bring them on, one by one, or all together, and see if I don't lay them flat on their backs."

"I confess I laughed too much," said Sancho. "But won't it make a good story?"

"I don't deny that it was something to laugh at," replied Don Quixote, "but it is not worth telling, for not everyone is bright enough to see the point."

"I have heard that when a great gentleman scolds a servant, he usually gives him a new pair of breeches to make up for it. I don't know what he gives him after a beating, but perhaps knights give an island or a kingdom."

"It may turn out that way," answered Don Quixote. "Forgive me. You know a man can't control what he does at first impulse. But don't talk to me so much from now on. In all the books of chivalry that I have read, there was never a squire who talked the way you talk to me. You don't show enough respect and I don't make myself respected. But remember that whether the stone hits the pitcher or the pitcher the stone, the pitcher comes off worst. And you will get the favors I have promised."

"All very well," said Sancho, "but if the time for favors never comes, what wages did squires earn in the olden days? Did they work by the month or by the day?"

"I think that squires never worked for wages, only for favors," said Don Quixote, "and yours are written in my will, because I am not sure how knighthood will work out in these terrible times we live in. My life is in great danger."

"That is true," said Sancho, "since even the sound of a fulling mill was enough to alarm so bold a knight as you. But I won't open my mouth to make fun of you again."

FOUR

THE FLYING HORSE

One evening, about sunset, Don Quixote and Sancho met with a group of elegantly dressed people on horseback. Foremost among them were a duke and a duchess returning home with their household after a hunting party. When they saw Don Quixote and Sancho they at once invited them to visit their estate, since they had heard about the knight's nonsensical adventures.

Don Quixote was delighted with this unexpected honor and wished to dismount in order to kneel before the noble pair. However, Sancho was not there to hold the stirrup. He had tangled his own foot in a rope attached to his packsaddle and at that moment was hanging upside down at Dapple's side, with his face on the ground. Don Quixote, who had noticed nothing wrong and expected Sancho to help him, flung himself off Rocinante's back and fell flat on his face. The saddle, which must have been loose, fell on top of him.

The duke and duchess kept straight faces and ordered their huntsmen to assist the knight and his squire. Nor did anyone else laugh, since all were under orders to treat these guests with the courtesy and ceremony described in books of chivalry. Don Quixote and Sancho went on with the duke and duchess to their castle, which was a real one and was not far away. Rocinante and Dapple received the hospitality of the stable, while Don Quixote was shown into a room with a splendid bed. Six maids came to dress him in a clean shirt, a scarlet robe, and a green silk hunting cap. When his armor was off and they saw his scarecrow of a figure they could hardly help laughing. However, he did not notice and sent them away. He was too modest to be undressed by girls. But after Sancho had changed the knight's clothes, Don Quixote allowed the maids to hand him soap and water and towels for washing his hands and face. They then led him into a great hall where the duke and duchess made him sit at the head of the table. They enjoyed the conversation of Don Quixote and Sancho so much that they kept them as guests for a week, always seeming to treat them with great respect, though at the same time allowing the ladies and gentlemen of their court to play a few jokes on the knight and the squire, who would believe anything they were told, no matter how absurd. When the duke learned that Sancho was longing to become governor of an island, he promised to give him one that he happened to own.

One day during the visit to the castle, a gigantic man with a long bushy white beard solemnly approached from the garden and demanded to see Don Quixote. He was dressed in a flowing black robe and was accompanied by a fife player and two drummers. In a deep voice he announced that he was squire to a highborn duenna, a lady of great virtue and dignity whose duty had been to teach and guard a young princess in a faraway land. Now the lady was in such trouble that she was known everywhere as the Distressed Duenna. She had come to beg Don Quixote's help.

"Let her come," said Don Quixote. "I will offer her the strength of my arm and the undaunted determination of my heart."

The giant squire withdrew. Again the fife and drums sounded and a whole procession of duennas came solemnly through the garden, all dressed in black, with white hoods over their heads and thick black veils over their faces. Behind them came the squire, leading by the hand a lady also veiled and clad in black from top to toe. She fell on her knees before the duke and duchess, who were sitting with Don Quixote.

"May Your Highnesses forgive your manservant—I mean hand-maiden—" she said in a hoarse, rough voice. "My misfortune has carried my wits so far away that I can hardly speak properly."

The duke and duchess responded graciously and made the strange duenna sit with them. Don Quixote was silent. Sancho was dying to get a glimpse of the ladies' faces.

The Distressed Duenna spoke again. "O most powerful lord and beautiful lady, before I tell you about my indescribable woe, can you tell me if you have in your company that most perfect knight, Don Quixote, and his squire of squires, Sancho Panza?"

Don Quixote rose and said, "O grief-stricken lady, I am Don Quixote of La Mancha, whose business is to help all those in need. Tell me briefly what is your trouble."

The Distressed Duenna threw herself at Don Quixote's feet and tried to embrace them. "O invincible knight," she cried, "your feet and legs are the very bases and pillars of knighthood!" Then she turned to Sancho and said, "O most loyal squire that ever served a knight-errant, beg your master to help me."

"Without all this flattery and all this begging," said Sancho, "I will ask my master to help you in any way he can, so go ahead and unpack your troubles and tell us about them."

The duke and duchess were bursting with laughter, for they had planned this adventure. They were amused by the clever acting of their manservant who was playing the role of the duenna, and also by the foolishness of Don Quixote and Sancho, who were swallowing the story as the gospel truth.

The lady went on, "It was my duty as the queen's oldest and first duenna in the royal palace to teach and protect the young princess. But a certain gentleman at the court persuaded me through gifts and flattery to let him make love to the princess, and since she soon fell in love with him, they were secretly married."

"The world is the same all over," said Sancho. "But hurry up, señora. I can't wait to hear the end of your story."

"The queen died of grief," said the duenna, "and no sooner was she buried than a huge and cruel enchanter, Malambruno, the queen's cousin, appeared above her grave, mounted on a wooden horse. By magic, Malambruno turned the princess and her husband into statues of a female ape and a crocodile. Then he pulled from its scabbard a scimitar with an enormous curved blade. He seemed about to cut off my head, but I pleaded with him for mercy, and at last he agreed to save my life. However, he forced all the palace duennas to stand with me and receive a penalty, which he said duennas deserved for their evil schemes and plots. At that instant we felt our faces being pricked all over as if with needles, and when we put our hands up to feel what was the matter, we found ourselves as you see us."

With this, all the duennas raised their veils and showed their faces, which were covered with heavy beards, some red, some black, some white, some grizzled. The duke and the duchess pretended to be astonished, and Don Quixote and Sancho were truly astounded.

"Such was the punishment which that wicked scoundrel, Malambruno, gave us," said the Distressed Duenna. "I wish he had cut off our heads instead of covering our faces with these coarse bristles.

Where can a bearded duenna go? Even if duennas use a thousand cosmetics to keep their skin soft, hardly anyone likes them, and who will aid them if their faces are covered with hair?"

Sancho Panza spoke up. "A thousand devils take you, Malambruno. Why did you have to put beards on these ladies? They probably can't even afford a shave!"

"I will pluck out my own beard," said Don Quixote, "unless I can somehow remove the beards of these ladies. Tell me what I have to do."

"The distance from here to my kingdom," said the Distressed Duenna, "is fifteen thousand miles by road. But if you travel in a straight line by air, it is only six hundred and eighty-one miles, and Malambruno told me that if I found a knight who would try to free me, he would send his marvelous wooden horse. There is a peg on top of the head, and by means of this he is guided and can fly as fast as if devils were carrying him.

"They say that this horse was made by Merlin the Wise, of King Arthur's time, and Malambruno uses him to fly all over the world. The best of it is that the horse does not need to eat or sleep or be shod, and he goes along through the air so smoothly that you could carry a full cup of water as you rode and not spill a drop."

"When it comes to smooth going," said Sancho, "give me my Dapple. He doesn't fly, but he can match any other beast on foot."

Everyone laughed, and the Distressed Duenna went on, "Malambruno promised that if I found the right champion to help me, the flying horse would arrive here half an hour after sunset."

"And how many can ride him?" Sancho asked.

"Two," she replied, "usually a knight and a squire, one in the saddle and one behind."

"And what is this horse's name?"

"He is called Clavileño the Swift," said the bearded lady, "Clavileño meaning 'wooden peg.'"

"I'd like to see him fly," said Sancho, "but don't think for one minute that I'm going to mount him."

"My worthy Sancho," said the duchess, "these are good people that ask your help and they mustn't be left in this condition because of your foolish fears."

"Sancho will do as I bid him," said Don Quixote. "Let the horse come, and I assure you that no razors would shave you ladies as easily as I will shave Malambruno's head from his shoulders."

"May all the stars of heaven watch over you, O valiant knight," exclaimed the Distressed Duenna. "O giant Malambruno, send the peerless horse Clavileño so that our misfortunes may end, for if we still have these beards when the hot weather comes, we shall be in a very bad way." She said this with such feeling that Sancho decided to go with his master to the ends of the earth if necessary to remove the woolly beards from the faces of the duennas.

Night fell, and Don Quixote was beginning to wonder whether Malambruno had changed his mind when, lo and behold, four wild men entered the garden. They were dressed only in suits of green leaves and were carrying a great wooden horse.

"Let him who has the courage mount this horse," said one of the men, "and let his squire sit behind. A twist of this wooden peg will carry the riders through the air to where Malambruno is waiting, but they must cover their eyes so that they will not be dizzy at the high altitude. When they hear the horse neigh, they will know that they have reached the end of their journey."

After the men had gone, Sancho said, "My master will have to find another squire to go with him. I'm no wizard to go flying through the air. Besides, six hundred and eighty-one miles is a long way. What if the horse gets tired? And what will the people of my island say if they hear that their governor is blown away by the wind? It would take us years to get back here on foot. I might never become governor of my island."

"Friend Sancho," said the duke, "go with your master, and I myself will give you your island, no matter how long it takes you to return."

"Say no more," replied Sancho. "Let my master mount. Cover my eyes, and when we're away up there, sky-high, I'll ask the angels to protect me."

With this, Don Quixote mounted Clavileño, his long legs hanging down, since there were no stirrups. Sancho climbed up behind the saddle and sat sideways to be more comfortable. The horse's flanks were very hard.

"If I remember correctly," said Don Quixote, "the wooden horse of Troy was full of armed soldiers who destroyed the city. Perhaps we should see if Clavileño has something in his belly."

"There is no need of that," said the Distressed Duenna. "Malambruno is not treacherous. May it be on my head if anything happens to you."

Then the two riders were blindfolded and everyone in the garden called out, "May God guide you, valiant knight! God be with you, bold squire! There you go, up, up, up! Try not to sway so much, brave Sancho."

Sancho was clinging tightly to his master. "How can we be riding so high," he asked, "when we hear voices as plainly as if they were right beside us?"

"Think nothing of it, Sancho," said Don Quixote. "This is no ordinary adventure and we may see or hear anything. Don't squeeze me so hard or you may throw me off. You have nothing to fear, for I swear I never had such a smooth-paced horse. It is as if we had never moved from the garden. All is well, and we have a fair wind behind us."

"It feels to me like the blowing of bellows," said Sancho.

This was the truth, since everyone in the duke's garden had a pair of bellows which they were pumping to make a breeze.

"We must have risen to the region from which snow and hail fall," said Don Quixote. "Above that is the region which produces thunder and lightning. If we go on up at this rate we will soon be near the sun's fire. I hope we won't be scorched, since I don't know how to control the wooden peg."

As he spoke, they felt heat. The people of the duke's household were holding poles with pieces of burning yarn hanging from them.

"We must already be in that fiery place," said Sancho. "I think my beard is singed. I want to take a peek."

"Don't do that," said Don Quixote. "Remember the true story about the man whom the devil carried through the air with his eyes shut. They went to Rome and back to Madrid in one day, and on the way the devil told him to open his eyes for one moment. He found himself so near the moon that he could have put out his hand and touched it. He didn't dare look down at the earth. So we had better not uncover our eyes. It doesn't seem long since we left the garden, but we must have gone a very long way. We are probably only gaining altitude before landing."

The duke and the duchess were much amused by the conversation of the two brave horsemen. To put a final touch on the adventure they now set fire to Clavileño's tail, whereupon the horse, which was filled with fireworks, blew up with a loud noise. Don Quixote and Sancho fell to the ground.

Much the worse for wear, they opened their eyes and were aston-ished to find themselves in the garden again. The bearded ladies had disappeared, and everyone else lay flat on the ground. Thrust into the earth at one side of the garden was a lance from which hung a parchment inscribed in letters of gold with these words:

The valor of the famous knight,
Don Quixote of La Mancha,
has brought to an end
the adventure of the Distressed Duenna.
Malambruno is satisfied.
The faces of the duennas
are once more smooth and clean.

Everyone in the garden now began to stir as if waking from a deep sleep, and the duke embraced Don Quixote, calling him the best knight in the history of the world.

Sancho wanted to see what the Distressed Duenna looked like without her beard, but none of the duennas reappeared. He was told only that they were now clean-shaven, without a sign of hair on their faces. The duchess then asked what adventures Sancho had had on the long journey.

"Señora," he replied, "when we were flying at the greatest height, my master forbade me to uncover my eyes, but I always want to do what anyone tells me not to do, so I lifted the blindfold a very little bit, next to my nose, and looked down. The earth seemed no bigger than a mustard seed, and the people on it looked the size of hazelnuts."

"Friend Sancho," said the duchess, "you couldn't have seen the earth if it was only the size of a mustard seed, since one man the size of a hazelnut would have covered it."

"True," Sancho admitted, "but we were flying by enchantment, and that's how I saw everything. I then uncovered my eyes completely and found myself so close to the sky that I could have touched it. And a mighty big place it is, I can tell you."

"And what about you, Don Quixote?" asked the duke.

"I saw nothing," said the knight, "but I knew we were close to the sun. Since the sky is far above that, we could not have reached it without being burned. Sancho is either lying or dreaming."

No one asked Sancho any more about his journey, for they saw that he would ramble on and on about everything that he had seen and done in the air, even though he had never left the garden.

So this was the end of the adventure of the Distressed Duenna, one that made the duke and duchess laugh for the rest of their lives, while Sancho had something to talk about for as long as he lived.

But Don Quixote said privately to Sancho, "If you want me to believe what you saw up there, you will have to believe whatever I see down here. And that's that."

FIVE

SANCHO'S ISLAND

The day after the adventure with the flying horse, the duke and duchess decided to play another joke on Sancho, seeing that he would believe anything. They ordered their servants and tenants to treat him with great respect, and the duke then announced that Sancho should prepare to become governor of his island, whose people were longing for his arrival.

Sancho bowed and said, "Sir, ever since my ride in the sky, when I saw how small the earth is, being a governor of a mustard seed doesn't seem so great. Could you give me a very small bit of heaven instead?"

"Friend Sancho," said the duke, "only God can give you a piece of heaven. But I can give you an island of good, fertile earth, and if you manage things well there, you can go from the riches of earth to the riches of heaven."

"Very well, then," said Sancho, "bring on your island, and I'll try to be such a good governor that I'll go straight to heaven, in spite of all the rascals."

"You will enjoy giving orders and being obeyed," said the duke. "Wait and see. This afternoon they will fit you out with the proper clothes."

"Sir," answered Sancho, "in my opinion it's good to be giving orders, if only to a herd of cattle, but however I'm dressed, I'll still be Sancho Panza."

"True enough," the duke agreed, "but your clothes should suit your rank, Sancho. You will be dressed as part lawyer, part captain, for both law and military command are necessary in the island I am giving you."

Just then Don Quixote came in and, hearing that Sancho was about to leave, took him to his room and made him sit down.

"Sancho, my friend," he said, "I thank heaven that Fortune has come your way before I have met her. I had hoped for good luck so that I could pay you for your services, but before that happened, all your wishes are being fulfilled. They say that good luck and bad luck come to all men. Here you are, a real blockhead, who doesn't work late or rise early; you are lazy, and yet merely breathing the air of knight-errantry, you become a governor with no trouble at all.

"Remember, then, that you have not earned this favor by your own merit, and pay attention to my advice, for high places are full of trouble and confusion. First, fear God. Second, remember who you are, so that you won't be puffed up like the frog that tried to make himself as big as an ox."

"I don't see what all this has to do with me," said Sancho. "Not all governors come from royal families."

"True," said Don Quixote, "so don't be ashamed to say you are a peasant. It is better to be virtuous and poor than rich and sinful. If

any of your family come to visit you, welcome them. If you take your wife with you, see that she learns as much as she can, and has good manners. Many a governor is ruined by a foolish wife.

"Be compassionate to the poor and just to both rich and poor. Don't speak harshly to the man you have to punish; the pain of the punishment is enough without adding insults. Remember that the culprit you have to judge is a wretched man, and as far as you can, show mercy, for the mercy of God shines more brightly in our eyes than His justice. If you follow these rules, Sancho, your days will be long, you will live in peace and goodwill, and when death comes in your old age, the hands of your grandchildren's children will tenderly close your eyes."

Don Quixote continued with his advice for so long that Sancho finally said, "Sir, all you have told me is good and useful, but what use is it if I can't remember it? You'll have to write it down for me.

A priest can go over it with me until it's hammered into my head."

"I have given you the best advice in my power," said Don Quixote. "God speed you, Sancho. I hope you won't turn your island upside down."

"Sir," answered Sancho, "if you don't think I'm fit to govern, I can give it up. Plain Sancho can live on bread and onions as well as Governor Sancho can live on partridges and capons. We're all equal when we're asleep, rich and poor alike. Don't forget it was you who put the idea of governing in my head. I'd rather go to heaven as plain Sancho than to hell as governor."

"By God, Sancho," said Don Quixote, "those last words of yours show that you are fit to govern a thousand islands. Try to do right whatever happens, and heaven will help you. Now let's go to dinner."

Before leaving, Sancho wrote a letter to his wife: "I must tell you, Teresa, that I am determined you shall ride in a coach as a governor's wife should. I am sending you a green hunting suit that my lady the duchess gave me. Make it into a skirt and bodice for our daughter. In these parts, they call my master, Don Quixote, a sensible madman and a wise idiot, and they say I am just as bad. In a few days I'll leave for my island, where I hope to make money, as all new governors hope to do. I will find out whether or not you should come with me. Dapple is well and sends his greetings. I will not leave him behind, even if they take me away to be Grand Turk. It worries me that I may like being governor too much, and pay up for it. But one way or another, you are going to be a rich woman and a lucky one. Your husband, the Governor, Sancho Panza."

Teresa Panza wrote back: "Dearest Husband, I received your letter and almost went mad for joy. When I saw the suit that you sent me, I thought it must be a dream. Who ever thought that a goatherd could become a governor of islands? I am anxious to come to court, riding in a coach. Think it over. No one here believes you are a governor. They all say it is some kind of humbug, or one of those enchantments that happens to your master, Don Quixote. But I just laugh and go on planning the dress I am going to make for our daughter. Send me a few strings of pearls if they have any in that island. I await your decision about my going to court, and may God preserve you more years than me—or at least as many, because I don't want to leave you in this world without me. Your wife, Teresa Panza."

Don Quixote wrote out his instructions, and Sancho got ready to set off to the village that was to be his island. He was dressed in a lawyer's robe with a military coat over it, and a cap on his head. Mounted on a mule, with Dapple following decked out in silken trappings and ornaments, Sancho was so happy that he would not have changed places with the emperor of Germany. When it was time to go, he kissed the hands of the duke and duchess. Don Quixote gave him a tearful blessing, and Sancho blubbered.

Before long, he and his followers, the duke's servants, came to a village of about a thousand people, living on land owned by the duke. The town officials came out to meet Sancho, bells pealed, and the people cheered. Those who were in on the joke gave him the keys to the city and proclaimed him governor, though privately they laughed at his strange dress and his fat little figure. Finally, they made him sit in the judge's chair, and the duke's steward said, "Sir Governor, anyone who rules this island has to answer difficult questions so that the people can see how intelligent he is and decide whether they will like him."

At that moment, two men came into the judgment hall, one dressed like a laborer, and one like a tailor, carrying a pair of scissors.

"My lord Governor," said the tailor, "we have come to ask for your judgment in a quarrel. Yesterday this man came to my shop with a piece of cloth, and asked if it was big enough to make a cap. I told him yes. Then he, thinking I meant to cheat him, said, 'Is there enough for two caps?' I saw that he was trying to trick me, so I said yes. Then he went on adding caps and I went on saying yes, till we got to five. Now he has come for the caps that he ordered. But he won't pay me and says I must either give him back his cloth or pay him for it."

"That's right," said the laborer, "but make him show you the caps."

"Gladly," said the tailor. With that, he brought his hand out from under his cloak and showed five little caps, on his four fingers and thumb. "There's not a scrap of cloth left over," he said, "and anyone can inspect my work."

Everyone laughed except Sancho, who thought for a while and then said, "This case can be decided easily and fairly. The tailor shall lose his work and the laborer his cloth, and the caps can be given to the prisoners in the jail. I don't want to hear any more about it." Again everyone laughed, but the governor's orders were carried out.

The next case filled the judgment hall with admiration. In came two old men, one of whom walked with the help of a cane.

"Sir," said the other man, "some time ago I loaned this fellow ten gold pieces as a favor, on the understanding that he would pay me back on demand. I didn't want to be hard on him, so for a long time I didn't ask for my money. When I finally did ask, he refused to pay. First, he said he never borrowed the money, then he said he had already paid it back. We have no witnesses, so I ask you to put him on his oath. If he swears before you that he returned the money, I will let him off."

"What do you say to this, old man?" Sancho asked the one with the cane.

"I confess that he did lend me the gold pieces," was the answer, "but if your lordship will lower your rod of justice, I will place my hand on it and swear that I have returned the money."

Sancho held out the rod, and the man with the cane stepped forward, handing his cane to the other old man, as if he needed two hands to give his oath. He then swore that he had given back the money, and his creditor said that he believed him, since he had sworn under oath. The debtor then took back his cane, made a low bow, and left the court.

But Sancho bowed his head and pressed his fingers against his forehead in deep thought. Then he ordered the man with the cane to be called back, and said to him, "My good fellow, give me your cane."

"Gladly," said the man, and handed it to Sancho, who put it in the hands of the other old man, saying, "Take this and go. You are now paid."

"Paid?" said he. "Is this cane worth ten gold pieces?"

"Yes, unless I am the biggest blockhead in the world," said Sancho. Then he ordered the cane to be split open, and out fell ten gold pieces. Everyone was amazed and declared Sancho to be a second Solomon. He replied that he had noticed how the man with the cane handed it to the other man before he swore that he had given back the money. Therefore Sancho had guessed that the gold pieces must be in the cane. Even a blockhead could sometimes guess right with God's help, said Sancho.

From the court of justice, Sancho Panza was led to a sumptuous palace where a banquet was ready for him in a great hall. There was only one seat at the head of the table, so Sancho sat down there. A man who turned out to be a doctor stood beside him, holding a rod in his hand, while servants put a lace-edged bib under Sancho's chin and brought him a plate of fruit. But he had no sooner tasted it than the doctor touched the plate with his rod, and servants snatched the food away. Another servant brought a plate of meat, but the doctor touched it, too, and it was whisked away.

Sancho was astonished and asked if all his food would be disappearing.

"Sir," said the doctor, "it is my duty to take care of our governor's health. The fruit was too watery, and the meat was too spicy."

"Here come some partridges," said Sancho. "Surely they will do me no harm."

"Partridges are the worst possible thing," said the doctor, tapping the plate, and away went the partridges.

"Then, please, Doctor," said Sancho, "pick out whatever you see on this table that will do me the most good or the least harm, and let me have my bellyful without your tapping it. I'll die of hunger if I can't eat."

"True, Governor," said the doctor, "but you should not eat that stewed rabbit, for the rabbit is a furry animal. You might have had some of this veal if it hadn't been roasted and pickled. But as it is, it won't do."

"What about that great dish?" asked Sancho. "It looks like an *olla podrida.* With all those meats and vegetables in it, there must be something there that I could eat."

"A mixture like that is not fit for a governor," said the doctor. "A handful of wafers and a few thin slices of quince will take the edge off your hunger and help digestion."

Sancho leaned back and stared at the doctor. Then he shouted, "Get out of here before I take a stick and beat every bad doctor out of this island, beginning with you. Get out, or I'll take this chair that I'm sitting on and break it over your head. Let me have something to eat, or let them take away my governorship. A job that doesn't feed the workman isn't worth two beans."

The doctor was about to take himself away when a horn sounded in the street, and the butler, looking out the window, announced that a courier from the duke had arrived.

The messenger entered, sweating, and handed Sancho a letter, which was read aloud to him: "I have just learned, Sancho Panza, that enemies of mine are about to make a night attack on your island. Stand on your guard so that you will not be caught by surprise. My spies say that four men have already entered the town to murder you because they fear your great talents. Watch out for strangers and eat nothing that is set before you. I will send help if you need it. Meanwhile, use your own good judgment. Your friend, The Duke."

Sancho was astonished, and everyone else pretended to be. "First, we must put this doctor in jail," said Sancho. "He intends to kill me by starvation."

"Nevertheless," said the butler, "Your Worship should not eat any of the food on this table."

"Then give me a chunk of bread and about four pounds of grapes," said Sancho. "I can't fight on an empty stomach, because the belly keeps the heart up. Tell the duke that I will follow his orders exactly. And tell my lady the duchess that I kiss her hands. And put in a kiss of the hands for my master, Don Quixote of La Mancha, so he will know I'm grateful to the hand that fed me. And now as soon as I get something to eat, I'll be ready for all the spies and murderers and enchanters that want to come against me or my island."

SIX

FAREWELL

Things never stay the same in this life. Indeed they seem to travel in circles. Spring is followed by summer, summer by autumn, autumn by winter, and spring comes again. Only human life moves straight forward and comes to an end, unless it is renewed in the next world. However, here we are thinking only of the speed with which Sancho's government came to an end and went up in smoke.

On the seventh night, as he was lying in bed with his stomach empty but his mind full of judging cases, giving opinions, making laws and decrees, he heard a din of bells and shouting. Thinking that the island was sinking, he sat up, confused, while drums and trumpets added their rattling and blaring to the terrifying noise.

Sancho leaped out of bed, put on his slippers, and ran in his nightshirt to the bedroom door. He was scared and stupefied by what he saw and heard. About twenty men were running along the corridor with lighted torches and drawn swords, all shouting, "To arms, Governor! An army of enemies has invaded our island, and we are lost if your skill and courage don't save us!"

"What's the use of my arming?" said Sancho. "I don't know anything about war. You need my master, Don Quixote. He'll get rid of the enemy in a flash. But I can't help you."

"Ah, Governor," called out one man, "why so fainthearted? See, here is your armor. Put it on and come with us to the marketplace. You are our governor and it's your duty to be our leader and captain."

"Well, then, arm me," answered Sancho.

At once they brought him two big shields with holes cut in them for his arms. They tied these on over his nightshirt, one in front and one behind, so tightly that the poor governor could not bend his knees or walk a step. They put a lance in his hand and urged him to march and lead them on to victory, calling him their north pole, their lantern, and their morning star. The poor governor tried to totter forward and fell down with such a thud that he thought he had broken every bone in his body. He lay as helpless as a tortoise in its shell.

"Prop me up at a gate," he cried, "and I will guard it either with this lance or with my body."

But the jokers had no mercy on him. They put out their torches and shouted and trampled over poor Sancho, banging on his shield. He pulled his head into his shell and lay there sweating with terror and praying for deliverance from his danger. Some stumbled into him, others fell on him, and one stood on him, shouting orders to the troops. "This way, men! Guard that gate! Knock down those scaling ladders! Bring grenades! Bring boiling oil! Barricade the streets with mattresses!"

Sancho, bruised and battered, listened to all of this and prayed, "Let the island be captured so that I can die, or at least be out of this torment."

At last he heard shouts: "Victory! Victory! Rise, lord Governor,

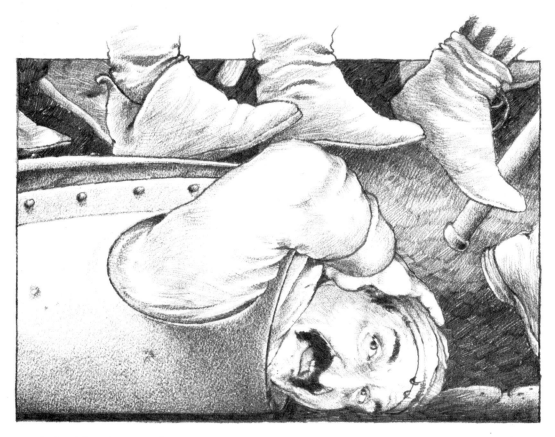

and divide the spoils your invincible army has taken from the enemy."

"Lift me up," said Sancho, in a weak voice. "I don't want to divide any spoils. But if I have a friend, I beg him to give me a sip of wine. I'm dying of thirst. And wipe off my sweat, for I'm dripping wet."

They wiped him off, brought him some wine, and untied the shields. When he was seated on his bed, he fainted away from all his fright and sufferings. The jokers were afraid they had carried things too far, but before long he sat up and asked what time it was. When told that it was daybreak, he began to put on his clothes, without saying a word. Then, followed by everyone present, he walked slowly, stiff and sore, to the stable.

There he found Dapple. Sancho embraced and kissed him, saying with tears in his eyes, "Come, old friend, partner of all my toils and troubles. When I was with you and had no care but to mend your harness and feed your little carcass, how happy were my hours and days and years! But since then, I have climbed the towers of ambition and pride where a thousand miseries and torments and four thousand worries pierced my soul."

As he spoke, he was saddling Dapple, while the others looked on without a word. Then, with great difficulty, Sancho climbed onto the donkey's back and said, "Make way, gentlemen. Let me return to my old life and rise again out of this present death. I was not born to be a governor, or defend islands from enemies. Ploughing and digging and pruning vines is what I understand. I would rather be free, lying down in the shade of an oak tree in summer, and wrapped in a shepherd's cloak in winter, than bear the burdens of a governor, lying between linen sheets and dressed in fine furs. Tell the duke, my master, that I came into this government without a penny and leave it without a penny, unlike most governors. Let me go and bandage myself, for I think all my bones are broken."

They had to let him go, offering anything he wanted for his comfort and convenience, but Sancho said that he wanted only a little barley for Dapple and some bread and cheese for himself. Wondering at his good sense and unshakable determination, they gave him a farewell embrace, and he embraced them with tears in his eyes and rode away.

He was within a mile and a half of the duke's castle when night fell, and he left the road to find a place to sleep. But by bad luck, as he was looking for a comfortable spot, he and Dapple fell into a deep, dark pit which lay among some old buildings. Sancho expected a long fall, but in about twenty feet Dapple struck bottom, and Sancho landed safely, still on the donkey's back. Thanking God, he began to grope around the walls of the pit to find a way out, but there seemed to be no escape. Dapple was in pain and was braying piteously.

"Oh," cried Sancho, "what unexpected accidents happen in this miserable world! Who would have thought that he who was governor of an island yesterday, with servants at his beck and call, today would find himself at the bottom of a pit, without a soul to come to his rescue? Some day they will dig my bones out of here, and Dapple's with them, and they will know whose bones they are because they will remember that Sancho was never parted from Dapple, nor Dapple from Sancho Panza." The donkey listened without saying a word.

At last morning came. Sancho found a crust of bread in his saddle-bags and gave it to Dapple, who seemed to appreciate it. Just then, Sancho discovered a hole in the side of the pit, big enough for a person to squeeze through. This he did, and found himself in a cavern where a ray of light came down from above. Beyond was an opening leading into a spacious vault. When Sancho saw this, he went back to Dapple and began to break away the earth around the hole in the pit until it was big enough for Dapple to go through easily. Leading him by the halter, Sancho moved ahead, often in the dark, and always in fear. When he had gone about a mile and a half, he saw a light shining from above and thought it must be coming from another world.

At this very time, Don Quixote was riding out from the duke's castle, exercising to prepare himself for a knightly adventure. As he put Rocinante into a gallop, the horse's feet came so near the edge of a deep hole that he would have plunged in if Don Quixote had not pulled on the reins, just in time. As the knight looked into the hole, he heard loud shouts coming from the depths: "You up there! Will anyone take pity on a poor sinner buried alive, an unlucky governor without a government?"

Don Quixote thought he recognized Sancho's voice, and shouted, "Who are you down there, calling for help?"

The answer came: "Who but miserable Sancho Panza, squire to the famous knight, Don Quixote of La Mancha?"

Don Quixote thought it must be Sancho's ghost speaking, so he called down, "As a knight it is my duty to assist the living, and I am ready to aid those in the world below as well. Tell me who you are."

"In that case," called Sancho, "you must be none other than my master, Don Quixote. And I am your Sancho Panza, and I've never been dead in my life. I left my government for reasons that would take too long to tell, and fell into a pit, and Dapple with me."

As if he understood Sancho's words, Dapple began to bray so loudly that the whole cave shook with the sound.

"I know that bray as if it were the voice of my own child," said Don Quixote, "and yours, too, dear Sancho. Wait until I go to the duke's castle and get someone to help you out of that pit."

The duke and duchess sent men with ropes and cables, and at last by dint of hard work Sancho and Dapple were pulled out of darkness into the light of day.

Seeing this, a student said, "So all governors should end, half-starved and penniless."

Sancho answered, "Eight or ten days ago, wiseacre, I went to govern the island they gave me, and I never once had my belly full. Doctors bedeviled me and enemies trampled on me. I never got a chance to take bribes or even collect dues, so I don't deserve to come out of it like this. But God knows me, and that's enough. I won't say more, though I could."

"Don't be angry, Sancho," said Don Quixote, as they rode back to the castle. "If your conscience is clear, let them say what they will. When a governor becomes a rich man, they call him a thief, and if he comes away poor, they say he was stupid."

"Well," said Sancho, "this time they'll put me down for a fool rather than a thief."

When they reached the castle, Sancho went first to put Dapple in the stable, because, as he said, the donkey had had a bad night. Then he went to greet the duke and duchess, who were waiting for him. He fell on his knees and said, "My lord and lady, because you wished it, and not through any merit of my own, I went to govern your island. You can ask them whether I did well, or badly. I answered questions, solved problems, and decided law suits, dying of hunger all the time. We were attacked by enemies and the people said we came off victorious, due to my strong right arm. I hope they are telling the truth. But my burdens were too heavy for me to carry, so I left the island exactly as I found it. I didn't borrow any money or take any profits, and though I meant to make some laws, I didn't do it because I was afraid they wouldn't be obeyed, so what would be the use? I left the island with only my Dapple, and fell into a pit where I would have stayed until the end of the world if it hadn't been for my master, Don Quixote. In eight days I learned that I wouldn't give a penny to be governor of an island or of the whole world. Let me go back to serving my master, Don Quixote. With him, I may eat my food in fear and trembling, but I get my bellyful, whether it's with carrots or partridges."

Don Quixote was thankful that Sancho had not made an even longer speech, and the duke and duchess embraced the squire with kind words. They were not sorry they had tricked him into the "governorship," especially when their steward gave them a full account of everything that Sancho had said and done in his "island."

Don Quixote now thought it was high time for him to leave the easy life he had led in the castle, and the duke and duchess gave him permission to depart. So, early one morning he dressed himself in full armor and descended to the courtyard, where everyone was waiting to see him set forth on his adventures. Sancho was mounted on Dapple with his saddlebags and provisions and was very happy because the steward, unbeknownst to Don Quixote, had given him a purse with two hundred gold pieces to pay for their expenses on the journey.

As soon as Don Quixote found himself in the open country, he felt all his knightly impulses coming back. "Sancho, my friend," he said, "liberty is one of heaven's best gifts. A man should risk even his life for liberty, and captivity is life's worst evil. You know how many luxuries we enjoyed in the castle, and yet they were no pleasure to me because I owed them to the kindness of others. Happy is the man who can eat a piece of bread for which he owes thanks only to heaven."

"All the same," said Sancho, "we shouldn't be ungrateful for two hundred gold pieces that the duke's steward gave me, because we won't always find castles to give us a night's lodging. We'll be staying at inns where they may give us a hard time if we can't pay."

Some days later, Don Quixote and Sancho reached Barcelona, where a rich and intelligent gentleman, Don Antonio Moreno, offered his hospitality. One morning Don Quixote rode out along the beach to take his exercise in full armor, for, as he said, armor was his only ornament and combat his only pleasure. He saw an armed knight riding toward him with a bright moon painted on his shield. As the knight came near enough to be heard, he called out, "Illustrious Don Quixote of La Mancha, I am the Knight of the White Moon, of whom you may have heard. I have come to do battle with you to force you to confess that my ladylove, whoever she may be, is more beautiful than Dulcinea del Toboso. If you will confess this, you will save your own life and save me the trouble of killing you. But if we fight, and I win, all I ask is that you lay down your arms, seek no more adventures, and stay in your own village for a year. During that time you are not to lay hand on sword, but to live peacefully and quietly, enjoying a rest that will benefit both your worldly affairs and your soul. If

you win, my head is at your mercy, my armor and horse shall be yours, and you will win fame as my conqueror. Give me your answer at once, because I must finish this business today."

Don Quixote was astounded at the arrogance of the knight's challenge. He answered calmly, "Knight of the White Moon, I have never heard of you, but I will make you swear that you have never seen the illustrious Dulcinea, because if you had seen her, you would know that no beauty can compare with hers. I accept your challenge. Take whichever side of the field you like, and I will take the other. May St. Peter bless the one that heaven favors with victory."

By this time the viceroy of Barcelona had heard of the strange knight's arrival, and rode out from the city with Don Antonio Moreno and other gentlemen to decide whether or not the battle should be allowed to take place. When he heard the details, he thought it must be a joke, and said, "In God's hands be it. Let the fight begin!"

The two knights thanked the viceroy, and Don Quixote, commending himself to heaven and his Dulcinea, wheeled his steed around. His adversary did the same, and they charged at each other. But the Knight of the White Moon, having the faster horse, met Don Quixote two-thirds of the way down the field, and hurtled into him with such force that without using his lance, which he seemed deliberately to hold straight up, he brought both Rocinante and his rider crashing to the ground. Then springing upon Don Quixote, he pointed his lance at the Don's visor and said, "Knight, you are defeated, and if you do not follow the terms of our agreement, you are a dead man."

Stunned and battered, Don Quixote did not even raise his visor, but, speaking through it, as if from the grave, said feebly, "Dulcinea del Toboso is the most beautiful woman in the world, and I am the most unfortunate knight. Drive home your lance, knight, and take my life, since you have already taken my honor."

"I will never take your life or your honor," said the Knight of the White Moon. "Long live the fame of the lady Dulcinea's beauty. All I ask is that the great Don Quixote retire to his village for a year, or until I release him from his pledge."

Don Quixote swore to fulfill all the conditions of his promise, as long as his lady Dulcinea was not injured in any way. The Knight of the White Moon then bowed to the viceroy and rode into the city at a canter. The viceroy gave orders that someone should find out who he was.

They lifted Don Quixote up and on raising his visor found him pale and bathed in sweat. Rocinante could not move. Sancho was speechless. All of this seemed to him like a bad dream or the result of enchantment. When he heard his master surrender and vow not to take up arms again for a year, his own hopes faded. He feared that Rocinante was crippled for life and his master's bones permanently knocked out of joint, though if his madness had been knocked out of him, too, that would be the one bit of good luck.

The viceroy sent for a sedan chair, and Don Quixote was carried into the city, while Don Antonio Moreno followed the Knight of the White Moon to an inn, determined to find out who he was. When the knight's armor was removed, he said to Don Antonio Moreno, "Sir, I know that you have come to find out who I am, and I have no reason to conceal it. My name is Samson Carrasco, and I am a student from the same village as Don Quixote. We all pity him and believe that he can be cured of his madness only by coming home to rest. Since he is the soul of honor, he will surely keep his promise. The success of my plan depends on his not knowing who I am, so I beg you not to tell him. He has an excellent mind, once he is freed from this nonsense about chivalry."

"Oh, sir," replied Don Antonio Moreno, "you are robbing the

world of its most entertaining madman. I doubt that your cure will work, and I hope it will not, because we would lose not only the good company of Don Quixote but also of his squire, Sancho Panza, who turns sadness into laughter."

"In spite of what you say," answered the student, "I believe things will turn out well." That same day, he started for home.

Don Quixote stayed in bed for almost a week, sad and moody. Sancho tried hard to comfort him, saying, "Cheer up, master. Thank your stars that you have come out of this with no bones broken. I'm worse off than you are. I no longer want to be a governor, but I would like to be a count, and I never can be one if you give up trying to be a king."

"Be quiet, Sancho," said Don Quixote. "My retirement is only to last a year, and after that I will go back to being a knight. I can't fail to win a kingdom, and I will make you a count."

Two days later, Don Quixote and Sancho left Barcelona, the knight mounted on Rocinante and Sancho on foot, with Don Quixote's armor on Dapple's back. As they drew near their own village, they came upon the priest and the student Carrasco at their prayers in a meadow. When they saw Don Quixote and Sancho, they greeted them with open arms and entered the village with them. They went to Don Quixote's house and found his niece and his housekeeper waiting for him, since they had already heard that he was coming.

Sancho's wife, too, had heard the news and ran out, half-dressed and with her hair uncombed, leading their daughter by the hand. Seeing that Sancho was no better clothed than when he had left home, she said, "Husband, what is the meaning of this? You look more like a tramp than a governor."

"Be quiet, Teresa," said Sancho. "Come home and I'll tell you things that will amaze you. I have brought money, and that's what

matters. And I earned it by my own work, without harming anyone."

"Bring your money, good husband," said Teresa. "However you got it, many others have done the same." She took him by the hand, and with their daughter holding on to his belt with one hand and leading Dapple with the other, they went home, leaving Don Quixote under his own roof. His niece and his housekeeper, who were good souls, undressed him, brought him something to eat, and made him as comfortable as they could.

All things come to an end, especially human life, and Don Quixote's life was no exception. Whether his sickness was caused by sorrow over his defeat, or whether his time to die had come by the will of heaven, he was struck down by a fever and kept to his bed for six days. The priest, the student, and the barber came to visit him, and his good squire Sancho never left his bedside.

They tried to cheer him, but nothing relieved his sadness, and the doctor did not expect him to live. When Don Quixote was told that he should prepare his thoughts for death, he received the news calmly, and said that he wanted to sleep. When he woke he said, "My judgment is now clear. All my troubles were caused by my continual reading of those books of chivalry, and now it is too late for me to read other books by which I might save my soul. My end is near, so let me confess my sins and make my will."

Everyone else left the room while the priest heard Don Quixote's confession. They came back with a clerk, and Don Quixote then dictated his will: "To Sancho Panza, whom in my madness I made my squire, I leave whatever money he has that belongs to me. It is my free gift, and if I had a kingdom, I would give it to him, for his honesty and faithfulness deserve it."

"Woe is me!" cried Sancho. "Don't die, master. Go on living for many years. It's the greatest madness to die without any reason. Get out of bed and let's go out into the fields. Who knows but we may find the lady Dulcinea waiting for you? If you are dying over that defeat, say you were unhorsed because I didn't tighten Rocinante's girth enough. Remember how in your books of chivalry knights often jostle each other out of the saddle. The one who is down today may be on top tomorrow."

But Don Quixote went on: "I leave to my niece all my estate after my debts have been paid. My housekeeper shall receive her wages and twenty gold pieces to buy a black mourning dress. I name our priest and the student Carrasco as executors of my will. And if my niece wishes to marry, she should find a man who doesn't even know that books of chivalry exist. If he does know and she still marries him, all I have left her shall be taken away and given to charity."

With these words Don Quixote fainted. He lived three more

days, and the house was in a turmoil. However, the niece continued to eat her meals and the housekeeper to drink her wine. Even Sancho Panza could not help being cheerful, for inheriting money helps to soothe the pangs of grief.

When death came for Don Quixote, the clerk happened to be present and said that he never had read in any book of chivalry of a knight dying so peacefully in his bed.

Such was the end of Don Quixote of La Mancha, whose real name and birthplace are not exactly known. All the towns and villages of La Mancha claim him for their own, as seven cities of Greece claimed Homer.

◆ ◆ ◆

He who wrote the adventures of Don Quixote also wrote a speech to his pen, as he laid it down: "Here you shall rest. Let no one else pretend to record further adventures of Don Quixote. For me alone he was born, and I for him. Farewell."

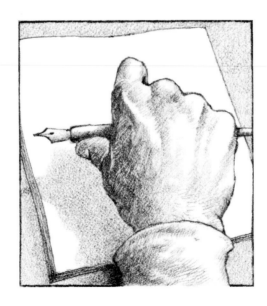